AUNTIE PEGGY'S WINDMILL

Auntie Peggy's Windmill

JENNIFER REES LARCOMBE

KINGSWAY PUBLICATIONS
EASTBOURNE

Illustrations by Toni Goffe
Linda Rogers Associates

ISBN 0 85476 444 5

Produced by Bookprint Creative Services
P.O. Box 827, BN23 6NX, England for
KINGSWAY PUBLICATIONS LTD
Lottbridge Drove, Eastbourne, E Sussex BN23 6NT.
Printed in England by Clays Ltd, St Ives plc

To my children,
Naomi, Duncan and Jane,
who shared most of these adventures
with me in Somerset.

CONTENTS

CHAPTER ONE

Auntie Peggy

Something very odd was happening in the kitchen. David and Emma crouched on the bottom step of the stairs, and peeped through the crack of the door. Daddy *should* have been sitting at the table drinking black coffee and reading the paper. Mummy *should* have been cooking their breakfast. But they were nowhere to be seen. Instead a fat little old lady in a blue hat was waddling round their kitchen, boiling milk all over the stove and burning the toast.

'I think that's great Auntie Peggy,' whispered Emma, 'The one who sends all the lovely Christmas and birthday presents.'

'I thought she lived in London, near

the Queen,' said David crossly. He wanted Mummy back and he wanted her *now*.

Yesterday morning Mummy and Daddy had driven away to a wedding, and David and Emma had played next door all day at Mrs Scott's house. After supper Mrs Scott's eldest daughter Jean had come home with them, put them to bed, and told them she would stay until Mummy and Daddy came home—very late that night. But now she had gone and there was no Mummy or Daddy anywhere in the house. Emma began to have a horrid wobbly feeling in her tummy. Suddenly Auntie Peggy caught sight of them, and when she smiled the feeling went away from Emma's tummy completely.

'Come and have some breakfast,' called Auntie Peggy. 'I'm afraid I've burnt all the toast. Would you mind chocolate biscuits instead?'

David said he did not mind at all and smiled his biggest smile.

'I expect you wonder why I am here,' said Auntie Peggy while they munched happily. 'Yesterday, when Mummy and Daddy were driving through London to the wedding, a big lorry ran into their car and bumped and banged them so badly they had to go to hospital in an ambulance.

They're all right but the doctor says they will take a few weeks to mend. So as I was setting out for a long adventure I told Mummy I would take you both with me.'

'I like adventures,' said David 'specially when you have chocolate biscuits for breakfast.'

Auntie Peggy's car seemed just as old and funny as she was, and in no time they were packed up and sitting in the back seat. Emma had her horrid tummy feeling back again, so she held Susie, her doll, very tightly. David wasn't a bit worried. He loved all cars, especially old ones, and he was holding Mummy's enormous shopping bag on his lap.

'What ever have you got in there?' asked Auntie Peggy.

'Nothing—yet,' replied David.

'You see, he collects rubbish,' explained Emma. 'He calls it treasure.'

'Good,' said Auntie Peggy squeezing

12

into the front seat, still wearing her old blue hat. 'I love collecting things too. I collected this poor old car years and years ago. I call her Garden.' It seemed an odd name for a car, but they didn't have time to say so before Auntie Peggy did something else which surprised them even more. She closed her eyes and turning to the empty front seat beside her she said, 'Please look after us and help me to drive well.'

'Is she mad?' whispered David.

'Probably,' replied Emma. 'But I think she might have been talking to God,' she added as Garden gave a gurgle and a snort and rattled off down the road.

Garden did not seem to like motorways much, and the lorries didn't seem to like Garden either. They all hooted and honked at her to go a bit faster. But she took no notice.

13

'Are we going to stay in a hotel?' asked Emma as they chugged along.

'No,' said Auntie Peggy, 'Guess again.'

'In a garage?' said David hopefully. 'Or a farm?'

'Nowhere like that,' said Auntie Peggy. 'Keep trying.'

'A cottage by the sea?' guessed Emma.

'On a boat!' shouted David.

'A castle, then?' suggested Emma.

'A caravan!' squealed David. But although they kept trying for hours, they never guessed. At last when the motorway was far behind them, they began to climb a steep hill.

'Poor old Garden hates this bit,' said Auntie Peggy. 'But we're nearly there now.' And just then they saw it. A *windmill*! And Garden stopped at last.

'But people can't sleep in windmills,' whispered Emma.

14

'They can in this one,' said Auntie Peggy, 'Come and see.'

Inside there were two round rooms, one on top of the other. The bottom one was a kitchen and sitting room all in one. There were no stairs— just a ladder going through a hole in the ceiling to one big bedroom.

'Does this windmill belong to you, Auntie Peggy?' asked Emma.

'Yes, but I only come here for holidays,' said Auntie Peggy.

'This is even nicer than a garage,' said David happily.

They unpacked and Auntie Peggy made some scrambled eggs for supper. When it was cleared away they all walked down the hill to the phone box to ring the hospital. A nurse told them Mummy and Daddy were feeling much better.

'Lovely,' said Auntie Peggy as she rang off. 'We'll just stand here and thank God right away.'

'I thought,' said David as they walked up the hill, 'that people only talked to God in church, not in cars and telephone boxes.'

'Well, he's with us wherever we go, so it always seems a bit rude not to talk to him often,' answered Auntie Peggy.

'We don't know God in our family, you see,' explained Emma.

16

'He knows you,' replied Auntie Peggy. 'In fact you two are very important people to God. I've been talking to him about you both ever since you were born.' David and Emma walked on very proudly; it was nice to be important.

It was rather like being the Three Bears at bedtime, because there were three beds in the windmill. One was very big, one middle-sized and one very tiny.

'David can have that one,' said Emma, 'because he is only six. I will have this middle-sized one because I'm eight.'

'And I'll have the big one,' finished Auntie Peggy. 'Because I feel at least a hundred tonight!'

David was soon sound asleep and snoring as usual. Emma lay awake a long time listening to the creaking of the old windmill and the sounds

17

of Auntie Peggy pottering about downstairs.

'I shall like it here,' she whispered to Susie, 'and I will be quite safe because I am a Very Important Person to God.'

Then Auntie Peggy came up through the hole in the floor and kissed her good night. Emma was asleep before she could see if Auntie Peggy took her hat off before getting into bed.

CHAPTER TWO

The First Adventure

'The windmill's on fire!' screamed Emma, leaping out of bed the next morning. The room was full of smoke and a smell of burning came from the room below.

'No it's not,' said David, who was already up and putting on his slippers. 'It's only Auntie Peggy burning the toast again.'

'I'm sorry!' called a voice from downstairs, 'But I always do it.'

'Don't worry,' called David kindly, 'we can always have chocolate biscuits again.'

Auntie Peggy was not like anyone else they had ever met. She was the only person they had ever met who wore a hat at breakfast time.

'Why *do* you call your car Garden?' asked David.

'Well, you see, I live all alone in a little flat in London and I've worked all my life in the same dull office. I call my car Garden because it's the only garden I've got. They say I'm too old to work now,' she added happily, pouring out another cup of tea. 'But I'm not too old to enjoy myself. I've been looking forward to this holiday. Most days we'll go out on adventures,' she continued with her little black eyes twinkling, 'but this morning we really must go into town to the shops. We can't live on chocolate biscuits.'

David thought they could, and he hated shopping.

'I'll sit here on this seat and watch the cars,' he said firmly, when later that morning they reached the doors of the supermarket in the nearby town. Because Auntie Peggy was not

20

like any other grown-up she did not make him promise to sit still and be good. She just waved her shopping list and disappeared into the shop followed by Emma, clutching Susie her doll.

As soon as they had gone, David was off into an alleyway that ran behind all the shops in the high street. It was full of dustbins, bulging plastic sacks and wooden crates. They were all full of wonderful rubbish.

'Treasure,' muttered David happily and began filling Mummy's shopping bag with all kinds of bits and pieces. He didn't seem to notice the flies and wasps which buzzed round him.

'Oh dear,' said Auntie Peggy coming out of the shop later. 'David's gone!'

'He'll come back when he's hungry,' said Emma. 'He always does.'

So they left the shopping in Garden and went and sat on the seat to wait.

'Susie is a beautiful doll,' said

21

Auntie Peggy, trying to stop herself worrying about David.

'Yes,' smiled Emma. 'Mummy made her and all her clothes for my birthday.'

The three of them sat on the seat in the hot sun, but still there was no David.

'He might have gone back to the car,' said Auntie Peggy at last. 'I'll go and look. And you go into the supermarket. We might have missed him somehow.'

They both disappeared and Susie the doll was left alone on the seat. When they came back, she had gone. Emma gasped and burst into tears. Susie was special because Mummy had made her. Mummy did not seem so far away when she could hold Susie tightly.

'It's time we talked to God about all this,' said Auntie Peggy, putting her arms round poor Emma. 'Please,' she

22

prayed, 'we're in a terrible fix. We've lost David and Susie. You know where they both are, so please help us find them.'

David had come out of the alley just in time to see a big redheaded girl hurrying along carrying Susie under her arm.

'Stop!' shouted David, dropping his heavy bag of treasure. 'That's my sister's doll.' The big girl began to run, dodging between the people on the pavement. David was much smaller than she was and his legs were rather short and fat. But he was angry by this time and that helped him to run faster than he ever had before. The girl dashed through some gates into a park.

'Stop her!' shouted David to some big boys on bikes. 'She's stolen that doll!'

'Stop her yourself!' they laughed, and one of them put out his foot and brought David crashing to the ground. Rage swam like a red fog before David's eyes, and he was off down the path with his fat legs going like the legs of a race horse. Far ahead he saw the redhead disappear into some trees. Through the trees he crashed and down some very slippery steps. There at the bottom was a square goldfish pond and beside it stood the girl. She was holding Susie by the hair and dangling her over the water.

24

'Give me back that doll!' gasped David. His face was all hot and red from running so fast.

'Come and get it if you dare,' mocked the girl. David never stopped to think if he dared or not, but putting up his fists like a boxer he rushed forward. The redhead waited until the last minute, and then as

neatly as a bull fighter, she stepped aside, leaving David to fall head first into the fish pond. The water was so deep that he could only just feel the bottom with his toes and every time he grasped the side to pull himself out, the big girl stamped on his fingers.

'I shall drown,' thought poor David wildly. 'And no one will ever see me again.' But neither of them had noticed a tall, thin man sitting on a seat, reading a book in the shade.

'That will teach you!' laughed the horrid girl, stamping on David's fingers once again.

'And this will teach *you*,' said a quiet voice behind her. The thin man lifted her right off the ground by the neck of her tee shirt. The girl twisted angrily free, but when she saw the thin man's face she let out a yelp of horror, dropped Susie and ran away as fast as she could.

With the handle of his umbrella the man pulled David out of the pond, and as he wiped him down with a large hankie, he listened to the whole story.

'She's going to feel very uncomfortable about this next term,' he said grimly. 'You see, I happen to be her headmaster.'

They walked together back to the seat outside the supermarket, and as Emma hugged Susie, and Auntie Peggy hugged David, the headmaster told the story of David's great bravery.

'Well,' said Auntie Peggy, when they had thanked the thin man yet again, and collected David's treasures from the alley, 'I thought we were only going shopping this morning, and having our adventures on other days.'

'We'd better not go shopping again,' said David firmly, while Emma whispered, 'Thank you, God,' over and over again all the way back to the Windmill.

27

CHAPTER THREE

Yes, No or Wait

'Auntie Peggy's odd,' said David one morning.

'She's nice-odd,' said Emma. They were sitting up in bed, listening to the sounds of Auntie Peggy making the breakfast down below.

'She's always saying, "I'm speechless" but she never stops talking all day long,' said David. 'Not even when she's alone. Just listen to her down there now.'

'But she's not talking to herself, is she?' replied Emma. 'She's talking to God, silly. She does it all the time. She doesn't kneel down or close her eyes, she just chatters to him as if she could see him beside her.'

That's what I mean,' said David.

'She's odd. But her prayers get answered. It's like magic really. I wonder if it would work for me?'

He thought praying was such a good idea he decided to ask God for a radio controlled car. One evening, very soon after, Emma and Auntie Peggy found him crying loudly in his bed.

'Do you want your Mummy, dear?' soothed Auntie Peggy.

'No!' roared David, 'I want a remote control car, and I've asked God three days running and it hasn't come yet. Why won't God answer *my* prayers?'

Auntie Peggy, trying hard not to laugh, said, 'If God gave you all the toys you wanted straight away, you would be so spoiled and horrid no one would love you and God couldn't bear that.'

'But God says "Yes" to all your prayers,' said David with a sniff.

'Oh no, he does not,' said Auntie Peggy. 'If he did you wouldn't be here now.'

'Why? Tell us,' said Emma edging up close.

'Well,' began Auntie Peggy. 'I was supposed to come down to the Windmill for my holiday the day before I came to your house. I got up at five in the morning and loaded Garden and switched on her engine— nothing happened. It was one of her bad days. "Please God," I prayed, "let Garden start so I can drive through London while the roads are still quiet." But God said "No", even though he

31

knows how frightened I am of traffic. So I had to go into my flat again and make a pot of tea and wait until 9 o'clock to ring my favourite garage man. He took so long to come, but Garden was mended at last and in I got again. But this time I couldn't find my glasses. I searched the car and then my flat and finally I prayed, "Lord you know I can't drive an inch without my glasses and if I don't leave soon I won't get there in daylight." I'm frightened of driving in the dark, you see. But still I couldn't find them. So I made another pot of tea and wondered why God didn't seem to want me to go to the Windmill that day. Then the phone rang.'

'Was it God?' asked David with round eyes.

'No,' answered Auntie Peggy, 'it was the hospital. Mummy and Daddy had been brought in too hurt to talk, but they had found a letter from me in

Mummy's handbag. It had my phone number on it, so they rang and asked me to come to the hospital at once. So I drove straight there.'

'But what about your glasses?' interrupted Emma.

'Oh, they were just beside the telephone!' laughed Auntie Peggy. 'When I got there I wasn't allowed to see Daddy, but I whispered to Mummy that I would bring you both to the Windmill, and take care of you until they were better. That's how all this adventure started.'

'And if Garden had taken you down here to the Windmill at five o'clock in the morning you wouldn't have been sitting by the phone when the hospital rang, would you?'

'And we would have had to stay with Mrs Scott,' added David, 'and she gets cross if we make a mess.'

'You see,' said Auntie Peggy. 'God always answers our prayers, but sometimes he knows it's better for us if he says "No" or "Wait." But they are answers just the same as "Yes."'

'Well, I suppose I'll just have to wait for my radio controlled car,' sighed David. 'But I hope when it comes it'll be a big one.'

CHAPTER FOUR

The Prize-Winning Boot

'The summer show's on next Saturday,' said Auntie Peggy one day.

'What's that?' asked Emma.

'Well, it's like a competition for people who grow vegetables or flowers in their gardens. Or perhaps they've made jam or knitted jumpers—all kinds of things like that. They give a prize to the biggest marrow, or the most delicious cake, or the rose with the nicest scent.'

'Could we go in for it?' asked David, thinking he might enter the frog he had hidden under his bed that morning.

'Well, there is a special competition for children—to see who can arrange the loveliest vase of wild flowers,' said Auntie Peggy.

'What's the prize?' asked David suspiciously.

'A silver cup,' replied Auntie Peggy. David thought that was very dull and lost interest at once, but Emma was excited all week.

Very early on Saturday morning they set off to collect the flowers.

'We'll have to be quick,' said Auntie Peggy, as they walked over the fields, 'because the judges arrive at the village hall at 11 o'clock and all the entries have to be there by then.' But it was not a good morning. David thought flower collecting was very silly. He also thought long, early morning walks were very tiring. He soon became grizzly and cross. At last when they were walking through a wood he disappeared altogether.

'Oh dear,' said Auntie Peggy, who was not used to boys. They searched among the trees and bushes, and at last discovered a delighted David, rootling round in an old rubbish tip.

'There are simply millions of treasures here,' he shouted, 'and I'm putting this one in for the summer show.' He proudly held up an awful old boot—not the wellington kind, just an old workman's boot, with the sole flapping off. Auntie Peggy and Emma kept on telling him all the way back to the Windmill that boots can't be put in for shows. 'You haven't grown it or made it,' they explained. But he

wouldn't listen and in the end they gave up. Auntie Peggy whispered to Emma, 'We'll let the ladies at the village hall explain it to him when we get there.'

Time was very short now and Auntie Peggy glanced anxiously at her watch several times as Emma worked away on her arrangement. There were no vases in the Windmill so she had to use a jam jar, but the arrangement looked very lovely as Emma carefully slid into Garden's back seat, holding the jar on her lap.

'It's just ten to eleven,' said Auntie Peggy, pulling the starter. 'There's just time if we hurry.' But it was one of Garden's bad days and there was nothing they could do to make her start. Emma burst into tears, but Auntie Peggy said,

'Quick! We could still get there in time if we run through the fields.' They set off in such a hurry they did not realise David was still wearing his bedroom slippers.

'No time to go back,' puffed Auntie Peggy as they ran. But the stones hurt his feet through the thin soles and the slippers kept falling off. At last one tripped him up completely and he landed in a heap—right in a puddle.

'It's no good,' panted Auntie Peggy, 'we're too late now anyway.'

Too late! Poor Emma. she had worked so hard on her pretty little arrangement.

'I'll run on myself,' she declared suddenly. 'I can go very fast on my own.'

'Take this card with you,' said Auntie Peggy, 'and give it to the judges. It's got your name and address on it.'

'Take my boot, too,' shouted David through his muddy tears, and because he looked so very sad, Emma did.

Down the lane she ran; but you can't go very fast with a dirty old boot in one hand and a jam jar in the other. She had to carry the card between her teeth. 'This is impossible,' she panted. And then she had a very good idea. 'I'll use the boot as a bag to carry the jar and the card,' she thought, 'then the silly old thing will be useful at last.'

It was ten past eleven when she arrived outside the tightly shut doors of the village hall. Inside she could hear important sounding voices and she knew it was too late. She sat down on the step, out of breath, tired and very miserable.

Just at that moment the vicar arrived with his little dog on a lead. He realised at once what had happened and he said, 'I'll take that in for you. I'm sure I can persuade them to accept it.'

It was not until Emma was half way back to the Windmill that she remembered that she had forgotten to take the jar out of the boot.

'We'll go back at two this afternoon,' said Auntie Peggy, as they had their lunch. 'We can see all the things people have entered then. All the winners will have a red card by their exhibit and we can get tea and buns there afterwards.' She talked on, but Emma was too sad to listen. The judges would never look at an arrangement in a silly old boot. Why hadn't she thought to throw it away?

Sure enough, when they walked into

the hall, there was no sign of Emma's flowers among all the other children's arrangements. Suddenly Emma wanted her Mummy and wished they had never come to the Windmill at all.

'Look, there's my boot,' squealed David suddenly. On a special little table by itself stood Emma's wild flowers, still inside the boot. Beside them lay a bright red card which said 'First Prize' and a beautiful silver cup. As they gazed in astonishment, a lady came over to them.

'Was that your entry?' she asked kindly. 'I had to judge the children's section and there were so many lovely entries this year, it was very hard to give the red card to any one of them. But it was such a good idea to use the boot that I felt you deserved first prize.'

'Well,' said Auntie Peggy, 'I'm speechless.'

Later they discovered Emma had

won a little brown envelope full of
money as well as the silver cup.

'I'll have the cup and you can have
the money, David,' she said. So they
were both happy. David used his
money to buy toffees at the village
shop and they all three walked up
the hill to the Windmill chewing
happily as they went.

CHAPTER FIVE

The Parachute and the Chocolate Cake

It was the postman who gave away Auntie Peggy's secret. He puffed up to the door of the Windmill one fine morning, with a bunch of white envelopes in his hand.

'Must be someone's birthday,' he said with a big smile.

'Not mine,' said Emma.

'Or mine,' said David.

'Oh well, must be your Auntie's then,' he said and rattled off down the hill on his bike.'

'Well, as a matter of fact it is my birthday,' admitted Auntie Peggy, as she burnt the breakfast toast. 'But when you're as old as I am you forget about birthdays.' David was horrified.

'But you must have a party,' he said.

'And a birthday cake,' added Emma. 'Our Mummy always makes us beautiful birthday cakes.'

'No one has made me a birthday cake since I was a little girl.' Auntie Peggy sounded quite sad.

'Then we will!' said the children firmly. 'We always watch Mummy so we know just what to do.'

Auntie Peggy agreed to weigh out

46

the ingredients, light the oven and then go up the ladder and have a morning in bed.

'We can always call you if we get stuck,' said Emma, as she tied Auntie Peggy's large red apron tightly round David's middle.

It is not as easy to make a chocolate cake as it looks. So many things can go wrong, and that morning most of them did.

'It'll be all right when it's iced,' said David hopefully, as he licked out the bowl. Carefully they covered the finished cake with the chocolate icing Auntie Peggy had left mixed for them and when they had stuck on some Smarties and some daisies from the garden, it looked quite nice. Emma put the cake into a large tin and hid it in the larder. By the time they had wrapped two mysterious parcels in yesterday's newspaper (because they had no

47

birthday paper) they felt very proud of themselves.

It had taken all morning to make the cake and it took poor Auntie Peggy most of the afternoon to clear up the kitchen. By the time it was done she was very red and hot.

'But she's not cross like Mrs Scott would be,' thought David. He wondered if anything would ever make Auntie Peggy cross.

'This Windmill is like an oven,' she said, 'We can't stay inside another minute. Let's take the birthday tea out somewhere and call it a picnic party.'

So they all scrambled into clean clothes, packed up the tea, and as Garden sailed down the hill Auntie Peggy said, 'I know what we'll do. I heard they are doing some parachuting over the old airfield today. Let's go and watch.'

The idea of people jumping out of

48

aeroplanes was most exciting, and when they arrived they were just in time to see a little plane circling high over their heads. Suddenly out of it fell the small figure of a man.

'Oh dear,' said David, 'He'll be dead soon!' But while they watched a great big white umbrella opened above him. Soon he had landed safely in the distance in a billowing heap of white parachute.

'We're too far away,' said David disappointed. 'I wanted to see what he looked like.'

'Well,' said Auntie Peggy, 'this air-field is hardly used these days, except for private planes and parachuting, so it can't matter very much if we drive Garden down that track. It'll take us right into the middle of the airfield.' But Emma could read the big notice which said, 'Strictly Private, No Admittance' and she felt a bit worried.

Over the rough track they bumped,

49

with David shouting, 'Go smoothly, Garden, or you'll joggle Auntie Peggy's birthday cake.' When they found a nice grassy place they stopped and spread a red and white tablecloth on the ground next to Garden. Carefully Emma lifted the cake out of the tin, and placed it in the middle as David arranged the rest of the tea around it.

'First you must open your presents,' said David when everything was ready.

Out of the first parcel came a purple teapot with no spout, that David had found in his favourite rubbish tip in the woods. Out of the other one appeared the silver cup Emma had won at the summer show. Auntie Peggy was so pleased she kept saying she was speechless over and over again. Just as they were about to start their tea they saw the little plane taxiing towards them down the runway. They were so near now that they could see three men in it, besides the pilot.

'They are all waving!' said David happily. 'They must know it's your birthday.' But Emma felt sure the waves had something to do with the 'Strictly Private' notice and she felt more worried than ever.

Up went the little plane high into

the blue sky and first one, and then another little man floated down. They could hear them singing and shouting as they glided down to land on the grass quite close to the car. The little plane circled above them. It circled again and then again. The two men on the ground began to laugh and shake their fists into the air

'He's chicken', they jeered. 'Too scared to jump.'

'Poor man,' said Auntie Peggy kindly. 'I expect it's his first try. I'm sure he'll manage it soon.'

At long last the third man appeared, but something was wrong.

'His parachute hasn't opened yet,' said David.

'He *must* remember to pull the string,' cried Auntie Peggy.

'Oh, shut your eyes! screamed Emma in horror.

'It's all right,' said David sounding rather disappointed. 'It's opening now,

52

but he's coming down a lot nearer than the others did.'

'Perhaps the wind has blown him off course,' squeaked Auntie Peggy. 'He's coming terribly close!'

'Out of the way!' shouted a frightened voice from above them. 'I'm going to land on you.'

'Quick, into the car,' shouted Auntie Peggy. They slammed the doors behind them just in time, for there came a bumpity bang on Garden's roof and a horrid scraping noise as something heavy fell off onto the ground. Suddenly Garden was wearing a great white hat as the parachute covered it completely.

'Horrors alive!' exclaimed Auntie Peggy as she forced her way out of the door and through waves of white parachute. 'Whatever are you up to?'

'I'm not quite sure, Ma'am,' replied the muffled voice of the parachutist. 'But I think I'm sitting on a chocolate cake!'

By this time the other two men had hurried up and were clutching each other, helpless with laughter, as their friend scraped lumps of gooey cake from the seat of his trousers.

'You shouldn't laugh!' said David's furious voice, as he pushed his way into the sunshine. 'Look what he's done to Auntie Peggy's birthday cake!'

'Well, you shouldn't really be here, you know,' said the pilot, who had landed the plane close by. 'But I'll tell you what we'll do. I must take this poor fellow up again when he's changed his trousers, and give him another chance to do a better drop. Why don't you bring your Auntie up with me for a birthday treat?'

As they soared over the airfield, catching sight of the Windmill far below them, they all agreed it was the best birthday treat anyone had ever had.

CHAPTER SIX

A Shipwreck and a Lost Hat

Another nice-odd thing about Auntie Peggy was the way she told stories. She told them all day long. Not just at bedtime, but in the car, when they went out for walks, and even during meals. When she found the children didn't know any Bible stories she looked rather pleased. 'I'll just have to tell you some, won't I?' she said. But she did not just *tell* the stories like ordinary people do; she acted them. She jumped on the kitchen table to be the giant Goliath, crawled under it when she was Daniel in the lions' den, and she marched round and round the Windmill as she told the story of Joshua at Jericho. Emma and

57

David loved it and agreed it was much better than television.

'She loves that old Bible of hers,' thought Emma early one morning. It didn't matter how early she woke up, Auntie Peggy was always sitting in bed with her big black Bible propped up on her knee. She had a cup of tea in her hand while her blue hat sat safely on the chair beside her. Emma had never seen any one reading a Bible before and she simply had to ask, 'Why do you do that Auntie Peggy?'

'Well, I chat to God a lot,' was the reply, 'but the Bible is God's way of talking to me. He tells me all kinds of things each morning.'

Emma snuggled down cosily in her bed as she thought about that. Then at last she asked, 'Is that why you're always so happy?'

'I'm sure it must be,' said Auntie Peggy. 'I would be a very lonely old lady if I didn't know God.'

'Our Mummy and Daddy don't know him,' said Emma.

'Your Mummy used to, when she was a little girl,' said Auntie Peggy sadly. 'And I've prayed every day since then that she will find him again.'

'God wouldn't give a "No" answer to that prayer,' said Emma, 'so it must be a "Wait" answer. I expect she's very lonely and sad in hospital lying there without us. Perhaps she'll start talking to him again while she's there.'

'Perhaps,' said Auntie Peggy, slipping out of bed. 'But now it's time for us to get up and have another adventure.'

She would not have got up so happily if she had known what kind of an adventure they were going to have *that* day.

It was all the fault of David's boat. Auntie Peggy had become as

interested in collecting rubbish as David was, and they spent ages gluing things together and making fantastic models. The day before they had found a large wooden box and, with some plastic bottles and margarine cartons, they had made a boat.

'We'll tie some string to the front of it,' said Auntie Peggy, 'and go down to the canal for a grand launching.'

When they reached the canal they decided to hire a rowing boat. 'We can tow your boat along behind us,' said Auntie Peggy, scrabbling in her handbag for her purse.

60

Unfortunately it was many years since Auntie Peggy had rowed a boat and they spent most of their time spinning round and round, or bumping into the bank. But David's boat floated proudly along behind them. Everything was going well until round the bend of the canal came a motor boat full of rowdy boys. They rammed David's boat quite deliberately and roared away laughing loudly as it sank.

'Horrid things!' shouted Auntie Peggy and shook an oar at them. David sadly watched his boat disappear into the black water, but a little bit of him was quite pleased to see that something had actually made Auntie Peggy cross at last.

'Look,' said Emma, 'The string's still floating, perhaps you could pull your boat up.'

But David leaned out too far, the boat tipped up and, with a terrible

61

splash, they all three fell into the water. Fortunately Auntie Peggy could swim much better than she could row, and with the help of some people in another boat they were all soon on the bank.

'Thank God no one was drowned,' said Auntie Peggy, as she sadly watched her hat bobbing away on the water.

It was not until they were back at the boat house, wrapped in towels and sipping hot tea that Auntie Peggy remembered her handbag.

'Oh no!' she cried in horror, 'I can't lose that. The car keys and the Windmill keys are in it. And all my money—and my glasses! I just *must* have that bag back!'

Poor Auntie Peggy. The shock was almost too much for her and she sat rocking to and fro, with tears splashing down her nose.

'We ought to pray,' Emma hissed into David's ear. Almost before they had closed their eyes, a young man stepped out of the crowd which had gathered round them and said, 'My friend often goes deep-sea diving. He only lives down the lane. I'll run and see if he can help.'

In a very short time he was back with a man dressed in a black rubber suit.

'I'll have a try,' said the diver, 'but I don't think there's much hope.'

They squelched along the bank until they reached the place where the shipwreck had happened. A crowd of interested people followed then and everyone watched fascinated as the diver put on flippers and a face mask, strapped his two air bottles on to his back, and slid into the water. Auntie Peggy prayed, and a man from the

local paper took a photograph. Then they all stood in silence for what seemed like hours watching the bubbles, and waiting.

Suddenly a black head appeared followed by a hand holding a brown plastic handbag.

'Hallelujah!' cried Auntie Peggy, and David nearly fell into the canal again with sheer excitement. The man from the paper took another photo of Auntie Peggy hugging the diver, and the next day the picture was on the front page.

'We're famous at last!' laughed Auntie Peggy, and when the ten pound note from her handbag had dried out they all went into town to buy her a new hat.

CHAPTER SEVEN

Lord Starcombe's Lost Treasure

The great day had come at last. Emma felt sick with excitement as she put on her best clothes and brushed her wispy brown hair until her head tingled. They were going to Starcombe Place.

Ever since they had arrived at the Windmill Emma had been fascinated by the stately mansion that stood below them in the valley. Sometimes when the sun shone on the great lake in the grounds the water looked like gold. So Emma pretended it was a fairy palace and told herself stories about the handsome prince who lived there. Auntie Peggy said that it all belonged to a man called Lord

Starcombe. He opened the gardens to the public one day every year.

'We'll go, won't we?' pleaded Emma, and now the day had come at last. But David thought it was a silly idea and there was a gleam in his eye which worried Emma. Yet the excitement of driving through the big iron gates and up the sweeping drive soon made her forget David.

Then everything began to go wrong. As they got out of Garden, two enormous and ferocious looking dogs bounded towards them. Emma was frightened even of little dogs, so she had to bite her lip to stop herself from screaming. But worse still, the dogs were followed by an equally enormous and ferocious looking man.

'You're much too early!' he shouted, glaring at them. 'I'm not ready for you yet. The fool of a woman who usually takes the money at the gate

had to go and break her leg this morning.'

I'm so sorry,' said Auntie Peggy, nervously. 'Would you like us to come back later?'

'I'd rather you never came back at all,' was the rude reply, 'but now you're here you might as well stay. Kindly have the courtesy to walk on the paths. This dry summer is ruining my lawns.'

With that he stomped back to the house followed by his dogs. David thought they looked as horrid as he did.

As they walked down the nearest path, Auntie Peggy whispered, 'I'm afraid that was Lord Starcombe himself.'

That was the end for Emma. Everything was spoilt. She had hoped to see a fairy prince, but he was just a cross old man and she wished they had never come. Even the golden lake was just a dirty brown, because the hot summer had dried up most of the water, leaving behind ugly, smelly mud. The afternoon was very hot and the garden was boring.

'I must get out of the sun for a while,' panted Auntie Peggy, sinking thankfully onto a seat in the shade. 'You explore for a little longer, then we'll go home and have a nice cup of tea.' She shut her eyes and was very soon asleep.

Emma wandered off to look at the peacocks, which strutted all over the dried-up lawn. She picked up a pocket full of tiny feathers, each with a bright peacock blue tip. She had a horrid feeling she was stealing, but she hated Lord Starcombe so much she did not care.

He doesn't deserve a lovely house like this,' she muttered. Meanwhile David was doing what David always did—looking for treasure. He had noticed the mud at the edge of the lake and was sure lovely things would be stuck in it. In he jumped, sandals and all, and the lovely gooey mud came right up to his knees. But he only found a few old conkers and some sticks, so he gave up and just wallowed in the cool mud like a happy pig. It was while he was picking up handfuls of mud and

71

letting it ooze through his fingers, that something dug painfully into his thumb. He squealed, thinking he had been bitten by a shark! He pulled a long pin out of his bleeding thumb and then suddenly realised he had found the best treasure of his life. At the other end of the pin was a brooch all covered with slimy mud. He waded into the puddle which was all that was left of the lake and washed the brooch carefully. When he finally rubbed it dry on the grass, he saw that it was made of gold, with tiny shiny stones set into it.

'Auntie Peggy, Auntie Peggy!' he shouted, as he ran over the peacock lawn, 'I've found you something lovely!'

Poor Auntie Peggy. She had been in a very deep sleep and when she opened her eyes and saw David—black from head to foot—she had such a fright. Clutching her heart, she said, 'I'm speechless!' three times over. But

because she was not like other grown-ups, she never mentioned the mud.

'Just look what I've found!' said David, showing her his treasure. Auntie Peggy put on her glasses and took a closer look, and Emma came running back to see what all the excitement was about.

'Goodness gracious!' said Auntie Peggy. 'Lord Starcombe *will* be pleased to see this!'

'He's not having it!' said David indignantly. 'I wanted it to be for you, to wear on Sundays.'

'Thank you, David,' said Auntie

73

Peggy gently, 'but that would be stealing. Everything here belongs to Lord Starcombe, and we must take it to him at once.'

'I don't want to go anywhere near him—or his dogs.' said Emma.

'Nor do I,' agreed Auntie Peggy, 'but I think we'd better.' So they all trailed nervously up to the house, while the mud on David dried to a wrinkly grey—'Like an elephant's skin.' said Emma. Even his hair stood up in stiff spikes.

Lord Starcombe was sitting outside his great front door, with a roll of tickets on a table beside him.

'I found this in the lake,' squeaked David nervously and he put the brooch into Lord Starcombe's hand. But the old man did not look at the brooch. He looked at David—right from his hair to the mud oozing out of his sandals—and his face turned an angry purple.

'How dare you wallow in my lake?' he boomed, and the two dogs growled and showed their teeth. Then he caught sight of the brooch lying in his hand and his face stopped being purple and went quite pale.

'Well I'll be...' he breathed. 'Follow me at once.'

Feeling very frightened, they went in through the door and across the polished hall to a vast dining room. There on the wall hung an enormous portrait of a lady. She was wearing a brooch remarkably like the one David had found in the lake. Lord Starcombe held up the brooch to the picture and compared the two.

'Well I'll be... ' he said again, and sitting down suddenly in a leather armchair, he looked as if he wanted to cry. 'This is the very brooch my father gave to my mother for her birthday long ago,' he said. 'He had the portrait painted to show her

75

wearing it. It was all my fault that she lost it and my father never really forgave me.'

'Did you throw it into the lake?' asked David, terribly interested.

'I was about your size,' went on Lord Starcombe 'and I was walking with my mother by the lake one day when I fell in. No one else was about and the lake was very deep that year. My mother saw that I was going to drown, so she jumped in to save me. She had a great struggle to get us both out and it was not until we were back at the house that she realised the brooch was gone. My father was furious. He had nine gardeners search the bed of the lake for a week, but it was never seen from that day to this.'

Half an hour later they were all sitting on gilt chairs, drinking tea out of cups that felt like egg shells and talking to Lord Starcombe as if they had known him all their lives. Even the dogs looked more friendly and no one seemed to care about David's muddy trousers or his elephant skin.

'When I was a boy,' said Lord Starcombe, 'I used to watch your Windmill from my nursery windows. It was still being used to grind flour in those days.'

After tea he showed them all the treasures in his house, and lots more portraits of his family. They all seemed to have died and Emma felt sorry for him. No wonder he was bad tempered if everyone he loved was dead. It was then that she remembered the stolen feathers in her pocket.

'If I don't tell him,' she thought, 'I shall feel uncomfortable for days.' So she pulled the rather squashed feathers out of her pocket and said in a shy voice, 'I'm afraid I stole these. I'm very sorry.'

Lord Starcombe said nothing, but crossing the room to a glass cabinet he took out a lady's fan made entirely of peacock feathers.

'This was my mother's favourite fan,' he said, 'and as she always loved honest people, I think she would have liked you to keep it.'

Before Emma could say anything he turned to David, 'Now it's your turn, young man,' he said. From a cupboard he took a heavy wooden box. Inside was a complete army of brightly-painted lead soldiers, cavalry horses and cannons.

'They were given to my great-grandfather by the Duke of Wellington himself,' he said proudly. 'But look after them—they could be quite valuable by now.'

Auntie Peggy began to say no, but Lord Starcombe quietly interrupted her.

'This child has done me a great

kindness. Let me give him something that gave *me* great pleasure when I was his size.'

As they drove home at last, Emma said it was the most wonderful afternoon she had ever had. Auntie Peggy said she was speechless, and for once David was as well.

CHAPTER EIGHT

The Last Adventure

'I've got a feeling in my bones,' said Auntie Peggy, as she packed a picnic lunch, that we're going to have an adventure today.' They had decided to go to the rubbish tip woods, because that always made David happy, and Emma wanted to explore the badgers' sets she had seen there.

'After lunch we could go down to the stream and paddle,' said Auntie Peggy, as they walked over the fields leaving Garden and the Windmill to have a peaceful day.

The morning passed happily and the lunch tasted good.

'It's hard to believe we've been at the Windmill for six weeks', said Auntie Peggy, as they munched.

'And Mummy and Daddy are getting better all the time,' said Emma happily.

'I hope they don't get better too quickly,' said David, through an egg sandwich. 'We ought to be going back to school next week and it's much nicer here.'

As they walked down to the stream, Auntie Peggy told them the story from the Bible about St Paul and the great shipwreck, and just at the most exciting part they all heard a strange noise.

'It sounds like someone in pain,' said Auntie Peggy. Throwing down their bags they hurried through the trees. At a place where the fields met the woods there was a double row of barbed wire and trapped on the top of this was a poor sheep. She was only a large lamb really. She had tried to jump the fence, but had landed on the two rows of wire, and now the sharp spikes were sticking into her tummy. Her head was hanging down and she seemed too tired to struggle anymore.

'If we don't get help quickly,' said Auntie Peggy, 'I'm afraid she will die. We'd only hurt her if we tried to get her down ourselves, so we'll just have to run for the farmer.'

Through the trees and down the little badger paths they hurried. 'We'll take the short cut down the high bank,' panted Auntie Peggy, holding her new hat tightly onto her head as she ran.

Now ladies of Auntie Peggy's age should never take short cuts down steep banks. The children slithered down on their bottoms, but Auntie Peggy slipped near the top and crashed down, landing in the ditch with a sickening crunch, her left leg twisted underneath her.

'Oh my!' she gasped, and slumped back against the bank with her eyes closed.

'Is she dead?' asked David.

'I don't know,' replied Emma, 'but I'd better find someone to help. You wait here and look after her.'

The woods were very quiet when Emma had gone, and David was frightened. When at last Auntie Peggy opened her eyes she didn't seem to want to talk at all. 'She *must* be dying,' thought David. Even the birds had stopped singing.

It seemed like hours before Emma came back, followed by the farmer and two ambulance men carrying a stretcher. The sheep was soon on her way to the warm farmhouse kitchen, and Auntie Peggy was settled in the ambulance with her hat and her handbag lying on her tummy.

David was quite happy again, because a ride in an ambulance when you are not actually ill is always exciting. But Emma's tummy feeling came back as the doors of the hospital closed behind them.

Two hours later they were still sitting in the hospital corridor on the hard hospital chairs. Auntie Peggy had been wheeled away from them on a trolley. They were surrounded by busy people rushing in all directions, and everyone seemed to have forgotten about them. They were both very hungry, and terribly frightened. Suddenly the double doors beside them burst open and a doctor in a white coat said, 'Ah!' in a very important voice. 'Your aunt has broken her leg in three places, and we shall have to keep her here for some weeks. The ambulance men told me you have no one else to look after you, so I have rung the police. They will decide what to do with you. Probably you will be taken to a council children's home. Sit here and wait until they arrive.'

With that, he strutted away down the corridor, leaving David and Emma to look at each other in horror.

'I don't want to go to a children's home!' whispered David. 'Shall we run away now and hide in the Windmill?'

'It's too far to walk there,' said Emma hopelessly. 'And anyway we haven't got a door key.'

They sat in silence holding hands tightly.

'Everyone who loves us is in hospital now,' said David 'and we're all alone.'

'Auntie Peggy said we were important to God,' said Emma slowly.

'She got it wrong for once, then,' answered David crossly. 'He's forgotten all about us.'

'Well, let's just try once and ask him to help us,' insisted Emma. So alone in that hospital corridor they closed their eyes and prayed.

'There, I told you so,' said David when they had finished. 'Nothing's happened. He only listens to people like Auntie Peggy who know him very well.'

The hospital chairs cut into the backs of their knees as they waited— too miserable even to cry.

Four people came through the swing doors at the end of the corridor. One was on crutches, and another walked with a stick. Emma and David glanced up to see if it was the police

87

and the next minute two shrieks echoed through the hospital.

'It's Mummy and Daddy and the Scotts!' shouted Emma, as they dashed down the corridor, 'God sent them just in time.'

'Gently does it!' laughed Daddy. 'We're only just learning to walk again.'

They all sat down on the hard chairs and gazed happily at each other.

'They let us out of hospital yesterday,' said Mummy. 'We wanted to give

you a surprise so Mr and Mrs Scott drove us down to the Windmill. But we couldn't find you, and then the farmer said you had all come here in an ambulance.'

'Auntie Peggy broke her leg,' explained David. 'They were going to send us to a children's home.'

'There, David!' said Emma triumphantly, 'I told you so! God does answer everybody's prayers.'

'Well, I'm still waiting for my radio controlled car,' said David.

'You may not have to wait *much* longer', laughed Daddy, 'because in the car we just happen to have a few parcels.'

When they had seen the doctor again, and explained to the police, they all went out to a cafe for tea. David's car was a really big one—a speed racer. It was just the kind he wanted. Emma had a paint box and Mummy said, 'We bought a

new handbag for Auntie Peggy. We thought she might need one when we read your letter about the canal adventure.'

Soon they were very full of sausages and chips, and before going back to the Windmill to collect their luggage, they went to say 'Goodbye' to Auntie Peggy. She was lying in bed with her leg held up in the air by a kind of crane, but looking much happier.

'I hate leaving you like this,' said Mummy, 'but we must get the children back to school.'

'Don't worry about me,' smiled Auntie Peggy. 'The Lord knew I needed a good long rest after all our adventures.'

'Before we go I must tell you one thing,' Mummy said. 'While we were in hospital we did a lot of thinking and talking. We want to know God like you do. When you're well, will you come and stay with us and teach us all about him?'

'Visiting time is over now!' said a fussy voice behind them.

'Well, I'm speechless,' whispered Auntie Peggy happily, as she watched them all walk away down the ward.